D1543975

Virginia Hamilton
The People Could Fly

THE PICTURE BOOK

Illustrated by
Leo and Diane Dillon

Alfred A. Knopf ✢ New York

We wish to thank Janet Schulman for the opportunity
to illustrate this story again as a picture book.

This book was done with love and respect for Virginia Hamilton.
Virginia brought magic, fantasy, and fairy tales to children who were rarely included in
these worlds. She inspired us as well as the young people she wrote for.
We were privileged to have worked with her on many projects
over a span of twenty years. Her lively tales and colorful characters offered a wealth of
images for us as illustrators.

The memory of Virginia will live for generations
with the legacy of her talent and love of "telling."

—*Leo and Diane Dillon*

THIS IS A BORZOI BOOK PUBLISHED BY ALFRED A. KNOPF
Text copyright © 1985 by Virginia Hamilton
Illustrations copyright © 2004 by Leo and Diane Dillon

Published in the United States by Alfred A. Knopf,
an imprint of Random House Children's Books, a division of Random House, Inc., New York.

KNOPF, BORZOI BOOKS, and the colophon are registered trademarks of Random House, Inc.

www.randomhouse.com/kids

Educators and librarians, for a variety of teaching tools, visit us at www.randomhouse.com/teachers

The Library of Congress has cataloged the hardcover edition as follows:
Hamilton, Virginia, 1936–2002.
The people could fly : the picture book / by Virginia Hamilton ; illustrated by Leo and Diane Dillon.
p. cm.
SUMMARY: In this retelling of a folktale, a group of slaves, unable to bear their sadness and starvation any longer, call upon the
African magic that allows them to fly away.
ISBN 978-0-375-82405-0 (trade) — ISBN 978-0-375-92405-7 (lib. bdg.)
[1. Slavery—Folklore. 2. African Americans—Folklore. 3. Folklore—United States.] I. Dillon, Leo, ill. II. Dillon, Diane, ill.
III. Title.
PZ8.1.H154Pg 2004
398.2'089'96073—dc22
2003025579
New edition with CD: ISBN 978-0-375-84553-6 (trade) — ISBN 978-0-375-94553-3 (lib. bdg.)

BOOK MANUFACTURED IN MALAYSIA
CD MANUFACTURED IN SINGAPORE

September 2007

10 9 8 7 6 5 4 3 2 1

Editor's Note

"The People Could Fly" was first published in 1985 by Alfred A. Knopf as one of the 24 tales in Virginia Hamilton's The People Could Fly: American Black Folktales. *The story has been anthologized more than any of her other works and is considered emblematic of her writing. After Virginia Hamilton's death in 2002, we felt that a fitting memorial to her would be a picture book containing just this tale, with all-new illustrations by Leo and Diane Dillon, the same artists who illustrated the original collection.*

The paragraphs below come from a letter she wrote to her publisher on May 4, 1984, while she was writing the stories for that collection. They provide perspectives in addition to those in her original Author's Note that appears at the end of this book.

"The People Could Fly": One of the mythical old tales in the tradition of "things that never were," as opposed to characters and events that were once actual. This tale might have been told as soon as the slaves came to America, or when a fresh bunch of "Africans" were brought directly to the plantation. This tale is in many ways timeless. Beautiful. I have taken out some of the repetition in this tale. Strange that in no version of this tale are the old man and the young woman given names. And in all black folktales, people have names. I have given the two central characters names. It seems reasonable to think that they would have had some sort of names. I believe that in one African west coast language, Toby was the name of a day of the week and quite common among slave names. In one version of the tale in a WPA collection, the Overseer is called Mr. Blue. But the slaves remain nameless. Perhaps the names were forgotten and not passed along with the story. Of course, in all other stories, the names do change as the generations who told the tales changed.

There have been persistent tales about blacks who fly. The last one collected that I know of was in the thirties. A man was said to walk faster and faster. Then he would take off. He was last seen flying faster than an airplane. There are stories about "wing" shops, where wings were purchased. I have come across more than 25 flying references, tales, and fragments. As you probably know, Toni Morrison ends *Song of Solomon* with her protagonist flying away. This tale, "The People Could Fly," both somber and uplifting, should end the book.

They say the people could fly. Say that long ago in Africa, some of the people knew magic. And they would walk up on the air like climbin up on a gate. And they flew like blackbirds over the fields. Black, shiny wings flappin against the blue up there.

Then, many of the people were captured for Slavery. The ones that could fly shed their wings. They couldn't take their wings across the water on the slave ships. Too crowded, don't you know.

The folks were full of misery, then. Got sick with the up and down of the sea. So they forgot about flyin when they could no longer breathe the sweet scent of Africa.

Say the people who could fly kept their power, although they shed their wings. They kept their secret magic in the land of slavery. They looked the same as the other people from Africa who had been coming over, who had dark skin. Say you couldn't tell anymore one who could fly from one who couldn't.

One such who could was an old man, call him Toby. And standin tall, yet afraid, was a young woman who once had wings. Call her Sarah. Now Sarah carried a babe tied to her back. She trembled to be so hard worked and scorned.

The slaves labored in the fields from sunup to sundown. The owner of the slaves callin himself their Master. Say he was a hard lump of clay. A hard, glinty coal. A hard rock pile, wouldn't be moved. His Overseer on horseback pointed out the slaves who were slowin down. So the one called Driver cracked his whip over the slow ones to make them move faster. That whip was a slice-open cut of pain. So they did move faster. Had to.

Sarah hoed and chopped the row as the babe on her back slept.

Say the child grew hungry. That babe started up bawling too loud. Sarah couldn't stop to feed it. Couldn't stop to soothe and quiet it down. She let it cry. She didn't want to. She had no heart to croon to it.

"Keep that thing quiet," called the Overseer. He pointed his finger at the babe. The woman scrunched low. The Driver cracked his whip across the babe any-how. The babe hollered like any hurt child, and the woman fell to the earth.

The old man that was there, Toby, came and helped her to her feet.

"I must go soon," she told him.

"Soon," he said.

Sarah couldn't stand up straight any longer. She was too weak. The sun burned her face. The babe cried and cried, "Pity me, oh, pity me," say it sounded like. Sarah was so sad and starvin, she sat down in the row.

"Get up, you black cow," called the Overseer. He pointed his hand, and the Driver's whip snarled around Sarah's legs. Her sack dress tore into rags. Her legs bled onto the earth. She couldn't get up.

Toby was there where there was no one to help her and the babe.

"Now, before it's too late," panted Sarah. "Now, Father!"

"Yes, Daughter, the time is come," Toby answered. "Go, as you know how to go!"

He raised his arms, holding them out to her. "*Kum . . . yali, kum buba tambe,*" and more magic words, said so quickly, they sounded like whispers and sighs.

The young woman lifted one foot on the air. Then the other. She flew clumsily at first, with the child now held tightly in her arms. Then she felt the magic, the African mystery. Say she rose just as free as a bird. As light as a feather.

The Overseer rode after her, hollerin. Sarah flew over the fences. She flew over the woods. Tall trees could not snag her. Nor could the Overseer. She flew like an eagle now, until she was gone from sight. No one dared speak about it. Couldn't believe it. But it was, because they that was there saw that it was.

Say the next day was dead hot in the fields. A young man slave fell from the heat. The Driver come and whipped him. Toby come over and spoke words to the fallen one. The words of ancient Africa once heard are never remembered completely. The young man forgot them as soon as he heard them. They went way inside him. He got up and rolled over on the air. He rode it awhile. And he flew away.

Another and another fell from the heat. Toby was there. He cried out to the fallen and reached his arms out to them. *"Kum kunka yali, kum . . . tambe!"* Whispers and sighs. And they too rose on the air. They rode the hot breezes. The ones flyin were black and shinin sticks, wheelin above the head of the Overseer. They crossed the rows, the fields, the fences, the streams, and were away.

"Seize the old man!" cried the Overseer. "I heard him say the magic *words*. Seize him!"

The one callin himself Master come runnin. The Driver got his whip ready to curl around old Toby and tie him up. The slaveowner took his hip gun from its place. He meant to kill old, black Toby.

But Toby just laughed. Say he threw back his head and said, "Hee, hee! Don't you know who I am? Don't you know some of us in this field?" He said it to their faces. "We are the ones who fly!"

And he sighed the ancient words that were a dark promise. He said them all around to the others in the field under the whip, "... *buba yali* ... *buba tambe*...."

There was a great outcryin. The bent backs straightened up. Old and young who were called slaves and could fly joined hands. Say like they would ring-sing. But they didn't shuffle in a circle. They didn't sing. They rose on the air. They flew in a flock that was black against the heavenly blue. Black crows or black shadows. It didn't matter, they went so high. Way above the plantation, way over the slavery land. Say they flew away to *Free-dom*.

And the old man, old Toby, flew behind them, takin care of them. He wasn't cryin. He wasn't laughin. He was the seer. His gaze fell on the plantation where the slaves who could not fly waited.

"*Take us with you!*" Their looks spoke it but they were afraid to shout it. Toby couldn't take them with him. Hadn't the time to teach them to fly. They must wait for a chance to run.

"Goodie-bye!" The old man Toby spoke to them, poor souls! And he was flyin gone.

So they say. The Overseer told it. The one called Master said it was a lie, a trick of the light. The Driver kept his mouth shut.

The slaves who could not fly told about the people who could fly to their children. When they were free. When they sat close before the fire in the free land, they told it. They did so love firelight and *Free-dom*, and tellin.

They say that the children of the ones who could not fly told their children. And now, me, I have told it to you.

Author's Note

"The People Could Fly" is one of the most extraordinary, moving tales in black folk-lore. It almost makes us believe that the people *could* fly. There are numerous separate accounts of flying Africans and slaves in the black folktale literature. Such accounts are often combined with tales of slaves disappearing. A plausible explanation might be the slaves running away from slavery, slipping away while in the fields or under cover of darkness. In code language murmured from one slave to another, "Come fly away!" might have been the words used. Another explanation is the wish-fulfillment motif.

The magic hoe variant is often combined with the flying-African tale. A magic hoe is left still hoeing in an empty field after all the slaves have flown away. Magic with the hoe and other farm tools, and the power of disappearing, is often attributed to Gullah (Angolan) African slaves. Angolan slaves were thought by other slaves to have exceptional powers.

"The People Could Fly" is a detailed fantasy tale of suffering, of magic power exerted against the so-called Master and his underlings. Finally, it is a powerful testament to the millions of slaves who never had the opportunity to "fly" away. They remained slaves, as did their children. "The People Could Fly" was first told and retold by those who had only their imaginations to set them free.